AF268914

To mothers everywhere.

Published by Mongoose Books

Copyright © Adrien Leduc (1987 -), 2023

Illustrations by Susan Golmazari
Translation into Chinese (Mandarin) by Zhang Xianjing

I'll Be There

我会一直陪着你

When the cold bites at your toes
and the frost nips at your nose...

I'll be there.

当
　　寒风刺痛了你的脚趾，
　　冰霜冻结了你的鼻子，
我会一直陪着你。

When things go bump in the night
and the shadows give you a fright...

I'll be there.

当
　　夜晚噩梦将你惊吓，
　　影子让你害怕，
我会一直陪着你。

When it's your first big day
and there's so much to say...

I'll be there.

当
　　你迎来人生第一个重要的日子，
　　我们有许多话倾诉给彼此，
我会一直陪着你。

School

When you're sick and need rest
to get back to your best...

I'll be there.

当
　　你生病需要休息，
　　恢复成健康的自己，
我会一直陪着你。

When your best friend moves away
and you'll miss seeing her every day...

I'll be there.

当
　　你最好的朋友搬去远方，
　　你对她的思念化成阳光，
我会一直陪着你。

When your other best friend leaves your side
and crosses the great divide...

I'll be there.

当
　　你另一个最好的朋友离去，
　　不知何时才能再次相遇，
我会一直陪着你。

Ginger

When you leave for university
to begin your life without me...

I'll be there.

当
　　你踏上大学的旅程，
　　开始自己的人生，
我会一直陪着你。

When it's your second big day
and you're about to become Mrs. Gaye...

I'll be there.

当
　　你迎来人生另一个重要的日子，
　　即将成为新娘子，
我会一直陪着你。

When it's your turn to become a mother
and give your deepest love to another...

I'll be there.

当
    轮到你成为母亲，
    将最深的爱给予另一个生命，
我会一直陪着你。

When you go through heartbreak
and wonder if it was all a mistake...

I'll be there.

当
　　你经历伤痛倍感失落，
　　怀疑自己当初是否犯错，
我会一直陪着你。

When you need someone to look after your finest creation,
to hug them and hold them and stoke their imagination...

I'll be there.

当
　　你需要有人帮忙照顾你最完美的作品，
　　牵着他们，拥抱他们，
　　点燃他们的想象力，无穷无尽，
我会一直陪着你。

And when I've aged, when I'm old and wise and gray,
when I have to remind myself to get the most out of each day...

I'll be there.

当
　我已变老，白发苍苍，却依然智慧灵光，
当
　我需要提醒自己充实过好每一天，
　仍怀有梦想，
我会一直陪着你。

For that is what a mother does, through good times and bad,
even when we're mad,
it's a love that never ends,
a love that endures life's twists and turns and bends,
and it's a love that protects,
from this life to the next...

因为
　　这是每一位母亲的使命，
　　无论时光喧闹或宁静，
　　甚至被生活重重一击。
这份爱永无止境。
这份爱承载着生命中的所有烦心事。
这份爱守护着你的今生来世。

About the Author
关于作者

阿德里安·勒杜克 (Adrien Leduc) 是一位终生作家和讲故事者，对青年和儿童小说充满热情。他通过各种机构和学校工作以及志愿者服务促进扫盲和教育。阿德里安（Adrien）和他的家人住在（加拿大）不列颠哥伦比亚省的维多利亚。

About the Illustrator
关于插画家

苏珊·戈尔马扎里 (Susan Golmazari) 是一位伊朗艺术家，在艺术世家中长大。小时候，她梦想成为一名宇航员，并且经常把自己画成宇航员。后来，她成了画家！苏珊（Susan）拥有艺术学士学位。自 2016 年以来，她一直从事绘画和插画工作。

About the Translator
关于译者

张娴婧 (Zhang Xianjing)是一位教育者和双语儿童读本写作者。她拥有英语教育学士学位以及英语语言文学和跨文化交流双硕士学位。张娴婧是加拿大不列颠哥伦比亚省翻译协会会员。

For more great reads, please visit
www.mongoosebooks.com